Reenactments from My Heart

Spiritual and Supernatural Civil War Fiction and Poetry

Shirl Knobloch

Reenactments from My Heart: Spiritual and Supernatural Civil War Fiction and Poetry

Edited by: Jennifer Sabatelli

Cover and Artwork by: Shirl Knobloch

ISBN 13: 978-0-9885171-7-2

Also by Shirl Knobloch: (available on Amazon.com)

✍ *Birdsong, Barks, and Banter: Adventures of an Animal Intuitive Reiki Master and Her Home of Misfit Companions*

✍ *The Returning Ones: A Medium's Memoirs*

✍ *You're Never Too Old for Fairy Tales*

Dedicated to my paternal grandmother, who said goodbye to her teenage son during World War II and endured life-long heartache after receiving the telegram that told of his ultimate sacrifice

Grandma Anna, I can only imagine the pain of your broken heart. The war took two lives away from me—my uncle's and hers. (Grandma Anna died before I ever had the chance to know her.)

Table of Contents

Prologue   1

The Battered Shoe   4

The Kindness of Strangers   9

The Peace of Home   18

Cries in the Night   20

Upon the Road   21

The Old Dog   23

In Her Bible   26

There Are Many Ways to Die   29

To Dance with an Angel   34

What's for Dinner, Jack?   37

Clouds   40

Taking His Place   49

Going Home   51

Seated with the Lord   55

Sorrow's Eclipse   58

Dignity and Deception   61

Blackened Skies, Blackened Bodies, Gettysburg   65

The Lady   68

The Loyal Rat   71

The Wind   75

Guardian Ghost   77

Blossoms in the Snow   81

Sounds   84

Socks of Love   86

From a Soldier's Heart   90

A Mother's Voice   92

Gettysburg Rain   94

Epilogue   95

Coda   96

Prologue

I own a Civil War farmhouse. I have seen photos of my farmhouse in Civil War books, so I know the way it looked in 1863. Most rooms are unchanged. As you enter through my front door, the formal front room awaits. This room was used to welcome important guests. It was the room to pay respects to the deceased; caskets were put in this room where, I am certain over the centuries, many have been placed at rest. Adjacent to this, the informal family room welcomed close acquaintances and relations into the home. Nineteenth century farmhouses often had two doors for these purposes, the formal and the informal one.

I know the name of the family who lived here in July 1863. I still use the closet where they hid their most important possessions, their flour and food, keeping all safe before the coming Confederate army seized them. I know the road on which this family must have fled as the Cavalry took over their farm.

I sometimes dig up old utensils and crockery in my garden, things the family and the soldiers might have used. Yet, I really don't know the feelings, the fears, the grief, and the heartaches this family and these soldiers must have endured those summer days in July 1863 and long after. I can imagine, but until one has lived through the horror, one can never really understand.

These stories seek to glance into their windows, their hearts, and their lives and help those of us who have never endured such horror understand a little more.

They are reenactments from my heart.

The Battered Shoe

Graham Kane and Martin Hale were childhood friends, growing up in a small village in Maine. They walked to school together, played together, and went to church dances together, their sights set on two of the town beauties. It was no surprise that the two of them left for war together in 1862, signing up for the same regiment.

Graham was physically stronger, but Martin lifted morale for both. His whistling as they marched urged Graham on, though they had seen things they never could have imagined. Martin was a sight to see marching; his oversized, old shoes with the floppy soles were laughable. But Martin was glad to have them; some soldiers weren't so lucky and marched barefoot. The two of them were indeed a sight to see......hair long, beards unkempt. They wondered if those town beauties would dance with them now.

Come summer of 1863, Graham and Martin were excited to be back on northern soil. Excitement over a big skirmish was spreading through camp; no rest was gotten this June evening. It was June 30, 1863. They were camped outside a quiet town in central Pennsylvania.

Martin was in a sullen mood, not like his usual, cheerful self. *"Graham, please take this letter and this photo and keep them safe for me. See that ma and pa get them."*

Graham didn't want these. He told his friend to keep them. But Martin insisted, saying that he knew the morning sun would be his last. The look in the eyes of his friend shot through Graham as sharply as a bayonet plunge. He took the letter and the old tintype.

July 1 brought horror. Martin was marching in the front line when the artillery cannon struck. Graham watched the whole line fall, the bodies of friends disintegrating into the explosion. He frantically searched for Martin, but there was so much whizzing by his head and so much smoke he could not see anything.

After the battle, Graham went back to a site more horrific than any he had seen since joining the Union forces. Bodies littered the fields so heavily that he had trouble not stepping on one.

When he reached the spot where the cannon shell had struck, his friend was gone. Nothing remained to bury; scattered, unrecognizable pieces of human flesh were all that remained of those with whom he once played cards and joked. Lying on the field was part of one oversized, old brown shoe with a floppy sole. The explosion had knocked it from his buddy's foot and sent it flying through the air. Graham picked it up and put it in his pocket.

Almost two years later, Graham came home to the tiny Maine village. He walked by the church, the dance hall, the general store, and the town circle and post office. Then he made the hardest walk of his life. He walked to Martin's front door.

His ma and pa hugged him tightly; questions about their beloved son's last moments flooded the air like bullets. They never found out how their son had died, only that his body was never found. Graham handed them the letter and the photograph. He had carried and delivered them as promised for his friend.

He watched as Martin's mother clung to that piece of paper and tin as if she were hugging her son. Then Graham knew what he must do.

"Martin was struck by a single bullet to the chest. He died peacefully in my arms with a peaceful smile on his face." Continuing with this lie, Graham then added, *"I buried him under a big pine tree."*

Tears streaming down their faces, the old couple thanked this boy for seeing that their son was properly laid to rest, at peace.

Graham had to go now. It was getting dark, and he had a few more miles down the road to walk before he reached his own parents' home. The emotions inside him were hard to contain; he needed to bid farewell to the Hales.

As he walked down the moonlit path, Graham stopped under a big old pine tree at the edge of the Hale farm and cried. He took a battered old shoe out of his pocket, reached for his pocketknife, and buried it in the soil.

The wind picked up. Its breeze seemed to carry a whistle as he slowly made his final march toward home that night.

The Kindness of Strangers

Jenna awoke to the brilliance of the Gettysburg sunlight. It was July 1, though 20 began the century, not 18. Gettysburg was her retreat. Friends from college thought it odd that a young girl would leave the city for the rural hills of Pennsylvania, but Jenna felt she belonged here. Here, among the bluebirds and hawks and hummingbirds that flew by, here among the peepers that sang, and here among the lightning bugs that twinkled like stars in the summer night.

She bought a rundown little farm with hopes of restoring it slowly back to glory. She delighted in rummaging the antique shops and flea markets and *side of the road treasures* to fill its space. Her farm was like a little time capsule, decorated as it would have been a couple of centuries past. All modern amenities were hidden away; even the appliances were locked away behind cupboards.

Although her space was still sparse and empty, she wasn't lonely. Her heart was full—not longing, like in the busy city—for Jenna was an old soul. This was her home; this is where she belonged. While other young women might be out on the social scene, Jenna was at her antique Singer sewing machine or with her knitting needles or on a stroll of the battlefields with her rescued hound, Blue.

On this July day, Jenna was extremely anxious. It was her first day in Civil War dress. She had sewn it herself and hand-knit the soft snood that covered her long, dark tresses. The summer morning was a lazy one; she was running late for the town festivities. Her farm was on the outskirts of town, close enough to be minutes away, but far enough to be her own quiet haven. She hurriedly dressed and fixed her hair.

Jenna soaked up Civil War history like a sponge. She read historical nonfiction, fictional stories, and fascinating paranormal accounts from eyewitnesses. She had wished to experience such an account of her own, but as of yet hadn't. Sometimes, Blue would look up in a quizzical manner; Jenna wondered what or who he saw. Perhaps one day she might find out.

Suddenly, the morning birdsong was interrupted by a knock on the door. A haggard looking young man, dressed in Civil War Grey, spoke softly. *"Morning ma'am...may I trouble you for a drink of water?"*

Hundreds of reenactors filled the town during these days. Many were tired and disheveled in appearance from sleeping outside. Others were elegantly dressed and coifed down to the precise type of button that adorned their jackets. All shared the same respect and interest as Jenna for this hallowed time in history.

Not quite sure about letting a stranger inside, Jenna led him to the side porch to a black wooden rocker and said,

"*Please wait here.*" She returned with the water, spoke a few words with the man, and went back inside to finish preparations for the day. So involved in her own thoughts, Jenna forgot about the stranger. Blue, however, did not. He was perched at the windowsill, intently focused on this trespasser.

Suddenly, Blue's barking caught Jenna's attention. She followed him to the door and out onto the porch. The rocking chair was empty, except for a tattered little journal and daguerreotype on the seat, alongside an empty glass.

She opened the journal. It read Joshua Jenkins. The last entry was dated June 30, 1863. *My body pains, I am tired......the march was hard, I saw my best friend breathe his last. May it end today..... Josh*

The battered daguerreotype showed the image of a young man, clean-shaven and not as haggard as the tired man whose thirst sought relief at her door. Chills traveled up Jenna's arms......

She placed the journal and dag in her purse and headed toward town. She walked down Baltimore, then York Street, heading toward the relic shop. Hesitating, she summoned up the courage to go inside. She had been in there once before browsing, but her pocketbook and heart were more comfortable searching out discarded items only valuable to her.

"Are these authentic?" she asked.

The proprietor looked them over quite intently. *"Yes, Jenna, how did you come upon these?"* he asked. *"Not many diaries have a photo with them. If you can locate records and prove the provenance of these items as belonging to Joshua Jenkins, they are quite valuable."* Jenna gazed silently, not answering his question.

"Would you be interested in selling them, Jenna?"

"No," she replied.

"Well, if you should change your mind, please let me know."

Jenna was certain she would not part with these treasures. Too anxious and mystified to focus on any anniversary events, Jenna went home. Blue was waiting and eager to soothe his companion's distress.

"I think we met one, Blue, a spirit....I wish I hadn't worried about getting ready and stayed a while with him." Blue looked up at her with soulful eyes that seemed to understand her words.

The sweltering heat was easing; the sun was setting, and Jenna carefully hung up her nineteenth century style garments. She entered the twenty-first century again, in jeans and cotton tank top, hair slung in an elastic ponytail, not curled into a snood.

As darkness descended over town, the only sound was the infrequent engine hum of tourists driving by and the night peepers' songs. *People were out looking for ghosts,* Jenna thought. *And now, I have met one,* she whispered to herself as she drifted off to sleep.

The next morning, all was back to normal at the farm. But the little diary and dag sat hauntingly at her nightstand. *So it wasn't a dream,* she whispered. *"Let's go do some gardening, Blue. Touching the earth always grounds me."*

The town was still buzzing, but the only buzzing Jenna heard were the bumblebees that whizzed by her head. Through the gleams of sunlight, Jenna saw a young man approaching her in the garden. Shielding her eyes from the glare, she saw he was about her age, nicely groomed and with a friendly smile. No car had driven up the road; he must have been out walking on this beautiful day.

"I didn't mean to startle you. Tom from the relic shop sent me this way...said you might have something I've been searching for. May I take a few minutes of your morning?"

Jenna instantly felt comfortable with this man. Something about him was familiar. Then she realized it—his face bore a close resemblance to the soldier in the daguerreotype! Imagining the dirt and beard removed from the image, Jenna could easily envision that this smile before her now was that of the soldier at her door yesterday.

"My name is Joshua Jenkins. My great-great-grandpa fought here back in 1863. He never left the battle. My family never found his body, but fellow members of his regiment told the family he kept a diary. I've been looking for that diary. Tom says you might have found it. Is this true?"

Blue was very relaxed; he didn't seem bothered by this stranger's intrusion onto his domain. Jenna asked Joshua inside and went upstairs to get the diary and photograph. When she showed him the old, worn journal and broken-cased daguerreotype, the look on Joshua's face was unlike any Jenna had seen before. It is best described as a mixture of relief and bliss.

Jenna could not keep what was not hers. She held out the treasures and placed them in his hands. *"They are yours."*

A look of gratitude flooded the young man's eyes. *"Thank you kindly, miss,"* he whispered in the same soft-spoken voice of one who came before him, *"more than you can ever know. I shall not take up any more of your morning."* With that, he said goodbye and walked onto the front porch, waved and smiled, and started walking toward town.

Jenna was a little wistful; this was someone who could easily capture her heart. If she were truthful to herself, though, he already had. She fought the mist that quickly clouded her eyes and looked downward at the ground. When she raised her head, he was gone.

"C'mon, Blue, morning is dwindling, and we've got work to do. I haven't time for foolish daydreams." Jenna and Blue went back to the garden, back to this morning and its labors.

A few days later, the Gettysburg paper was delivered to her mailbox. She had missed all the anniversary events, and she was eager to see the pictures and news articles. She quickly retrieved it and sat outside on the front porch to read the news.

Turning to the second page, a small article caught her eye and made her gasp in sorrow. *Young Reenactor Killed in a Head-on Collision.* How sad, Jenna thought, to die in such circumstances. Even more so, to be traveling to a Civil War reenactment where so many other lives were cut short by violence. Jenna thought this so heart wrenching.

Reading further on, the article stated, *"Joshua Jenkins, 26, was killed instantly when his vehicle burst into flames upon impact. This young reenactor was the descendant of Joshua Jenkins, his namesake. The elder Jenkins, a member of the* reserve artillery battalion in Longstreet's Corps, did not survive the battle of Gettysburg. His body was never located and brought home to rest. His diary and daguerreotype were recovered years later in a collector's estate and returned to the Jenkins family."

Young Joshua was a dedicated reenactor. He prided himself on his accuracy and devotion to his great-great-grandfather's memory and always carried his diary and photograph with him during reenactments. Joshua treasured them; he would tell anyone he showed them to, *"These will remain with me forever, for they are mine."* Sadly, the diary and daguerreotype were destroyed in the vehicle fire along with Joshua's precious life.

Jenna took a deep breath to quiet the whirlwind in her head. In her mind, she remembered a Bible phrase: *Be not forgetful to entertain strangers: for thereby some have entertained angels unawares.* Did Joshua's great-great-grandpa return to leave his diary and daguerreotype for his young grandson's spirit, unable to rest without them? Jenna believed so.

"Well, Blue, it seems that two angels chose to visit our farm. May they walk these fields together now in peace."

The Peace of Home

It was a sad morning on a little farm in Maryland. The war had come, and eighteen-year-old Matt was packing up his bag to set out for adventure and manhood. His mother had knit him two pairs of warm socks to keep his feet dry. Little chance of that in the long days of marching that awaited, through swamps, rain, and snow.

His older brother couldn't join in the fight; he had been disabled in a farm accident. To Matt, he gave a fine whittling knife, to carve away the hours between *adventures.*

Matt's baby sister, Lizzie, was especially blue; she and Matt had a special bond. She searched through her sparse possessions for something to give him. Under her bed, she kept a tiny wooden box filled with treasures...a piece of fine lace, a fancy doll dress mama had sewn for her, a button off her daddy's shirt that mama gave her after he died, and a small rock with tiny, glittering fragments that shone like stars in the sun. This was her wishing rock. She found it on one of her walks around the edge of the farm.

"Take this, Matt. It is my wishing stone. I wish for you to come home safely. Each time you look at it, wish on the sparkling stars within it and feel the ground of home upon which it once lay. Look up in the sky and make a wish on the stars that shine on our farm, too, that same night."

Matt was speechless, so touched by his tiny sister's gesture. He put the stone in his pocket, alongside his worn Bible.

He carried that stone through the wilderness. He held onto it in the darkness as he heard the dying cry out in the night. He carried it in his breast pocket beside a tiny, whittled horse he was carving to give to his little sister. He carried it to Antietam where he placed it in a dying friend's hands and told him to touch the ground of home and be at peace.

And he cried into it as he read the letter of Lizzie's sudden illness and death.

They found Matt on Culp's Hill, his bloated body unrecognizable. They took his whittling knife. They took his torn, dirty socks. They took his Bible for a souvenir. All they left was a tiny stone in his chest pocket and a piece of whittled wood that looked like it might become a horse.

As the dirt covered him, that tiny stone would be the only peace of home to lie upon him.

Cries in the Night

When you lay upon the damp earth and listen to the
screams.......

What matter if those screams come from a Kentucky boy
or a Pennsylvania General?

Does the thirst for water not quench a Northern mouth as
deeply as one suckled below the Mason-Dixon Line?

Does a mother mourn differently when she looks out into the
night and sees the Mississippi River or the Hudson?

Does fear not penetrate the skin of one clad in blue as deeply
as one wrapped in grey?

When you listen to cries in the night.......

Are they any different from the ones coming from your own
soul?

What matters which side, which reason.......when cries in the
night all lead to the same decaying death in the sunlight.

Upon the Road

I look out my farmhouse window
Upon the road
How many......
How many soldiers marched?
How many horses galloped?
How many made their final march
Upon this road
Past my farm?
My farm
A place of rest for thousands
A headquarters
A haven
Thousands of men
Thousands of horses
One Brigadier General
Some well
Some sick
All tired
All fearful
Some clutching letters from home
All clutching rifles
Some whistling
Some singing battle tunes
Some moaning in pain and agony
Some sleeping
Some unable to sleep
All waiting till the next battle
All waiting for the agony to end
All waiting for the sickness to end
All waiting for the fear to end
All waiting till the war's end
All waiting to walk home
Upon this road
Some made it home

Some didn't
And I often look out my window
Upon this Gettysburg road
And wonder.......
What lies buried beneath?
What fear,
What pain,
What sadness
Lingers in the air that hovers over
And permeates the atmosphere
Waiting upon this road?

The Old Dog

They grew up together
They roamed the woods of home
They went fishing together
They ran races together
In the soft fields and soft sunlight
Of youth
His was the furry shoulder to cry on
When life was sad
He was the buddy to run to
When chores were over.
The boy knew he was too old to come
But he couldn't stop him.
So together
They set off for war.
The old dog's bones were brittle
Marching took its toll.
The rain and cold brought illness
Upon his tired body.
But love gives strength
Till the body takes its final breath
Three months
He kept marching.
Till his paws were red and swollen
Till his joints were wracked with pain
Till his clouded eyes hurt
In the harsh sun's glare
Right beside the boy.
The nights,
He kept him warm.
The days,
He kept him safe.
Until his tired body could walk no more.
Then
The boy laid him to rest

And cried.
The boy kept marching.
His tired bones were aching.
His worn out body sick.
But he had to keep his brothers safe.
Until
The bullet came.
And he could march no more.
They carried him
To the hospital tent.
The doctor said it would not be long
Delirium....
He kept seeing him
The old dog
Try to keep him comfortable
So they did
Until the end
Then
They laid him to rest
And saw
The paw prints
On his grave

In Her Bible

I was seven years old when my pa went to war. I didn't understand why then. Part of me still doesn't understand today, and I am twice as old as he was when he left me, my baby brother, ma, and grandpa.

Grandpa didn't want him to go. He would have gone in his place, but pa said he was too old and lame. I would have to help ma and be a little man around the house.

Ma cried when pa left. She didn't sing us songs like before. The house was a lot quieter.

After my brother and I were tucked in our bed, ma would sit by the fire or oil lamp and write pa a letter each night. Each night, every night, ma would write. Sometimes, she thought I was sleeping, but I wasn't. I would watch her fold the paper, bring it to her lips, and kiss it before sealing it up in the envelope.

Pa's letters came, too. Ma would read us most; she said some things were just for her and pa to write. And each and every letter had a little dried flower or leaf that pa picked up on his marches in the fields. Ma picked each one up so gently and let us look but never touch. Then, she pressed each one in her Bible page. Sometimes, it would be a while before a letter came again from pa. But each time, a tiny blossom or dried leaf would be wrapped inside the paper.

Pa never came home. Ma said he died a hero. There was an article in the town paper about him. Ma placed that in her Bible, too.

All the rest of her life, ma kept those flowers in her Bible. The blossoms were brittle, the leaves crinkled and torn, but ma treasured them more than any fine piece of jewelry I gave her when I grew up.

When ma died, I took that Bible. I kept the newspaper article about pa but not the blossoms. I wrapped them in a piece of soft fabric and placed them in her clasped hands before they closed her casket. No other funeral bouquet was necessary or more beautiful than those tiny, crumpled blooms.

There Are Many Ways to Die

Charles and Augusta were sweethearts, but wedding plans were interrupted by war. All the boys and men from the small Mississippi town where they had grown up together were laying down their plows and picking up rifles, setting off to join the nearest regiment.

Charles' parents had died when he was young; he was raised by an elderly aunt and uncle. His aunt had passed two years before. His uncle remained, a strict and abusive man. Charles would not miss him. Charles had to enlist; it was a matter of Southern pride. Augusta's brother, Tyler, would join him.

The couple's last night together was spent looking up at the stars in the warm Mississippi evening. He gave his sweetheart a little gold ring—his mother's. She gave him a locket with one long, curled lock of hair.

Most of the town's men were gone. Augusta's dad had died some years before, and her brother had helped manage their small farm. Now, she and her mother would have to manage on their own, with few supplies and few farm animals to sustain them.

Charles and Tyler faced several long, hard months before their first skirmish revealed the true horrors of war. They watched men die, some quickly, some in agonizing slowness on the battlefield at night.

Charles and Tyler wrote back home, but soon, correspondence became impossible. Months would pass before any news could be exchanged.

There are many ways to die, and Charles and Tyler saw more than they could have imagined. And then, Charles saw Tyler die, his insides sprawled across the ground, his eyes paralyzed in a moment of terror. Charles closed his friend's eyes, but his own would never be blinded to the memory of that moment.

He went on fighting. He suffered shrapnel wounds to his face—gone were the boyish good looks and carefree spirit. That Mississippi boy had long since perished.

In Mississippi, horrors of their own were coming to the fields where Augusta and her mother toiled. Augusta was a beauty, a dangerous thing for a young girl only protected by an aging mother.

The soldiers came. They killed the farm animals, they killed her mother, and in the process, they killed Augusta. They killed her spirit and soul and caused a death just as brutal as if they had taken her mortal breath. They destroyed a young girl's sense of worth and dignity and destroyed all her dreams of a future with Charles.

When Augusta's letters stopped, Charles worried but kept hoping it was because of the war. He even sent a letter to his uncle, knowing he could not read or write very well, but hoping he would have someone check up on his beloved. No answer came.

Seventeen months later, Charles returned home. Augusta's farm was abandoned, the barn destroyed by fire. In the yard stood two wooden crosses. One bore the name of Augusta's father. Charles had recognized that one. But there was another. Charles' heart stood still for a moment, fearing it would have "Augusta" written upon it. It was her mother's name instead.

Charles walked on further, toward his uncle's place. Nothing and no one remained. Not much of his Mississippi hometown was left. People were gone, homes were burnt, and fields were barren, much like Charles' heart.

He spent the next few years a lost soul, his only companion a liquor bottle or brothel maid. Working women didn't pity his face or shun his disfigurement; money was the only thing they were interested in, not the story of a boy killed by war.

Charles preferred the anonymity of the big city. Con games and alcohol flowed with abundance there. It was 1868.

Charles had drifted into New Orleans. With money gotten in questionable ways, he headed first to the tavern, then to the brothel.

Then, to her room.

She didn't recognize him. Gone was the rosy-cheeked farm boy full of hopes and dreams. In his place stood the sallow, sunken shell of a man.

She extended her hand out to pull him over to the bed. Then, he saw the ring. He sat down, took out a small locket from his breast pocket, and gazed at the beautiful blonde tress of youth and innocence.

Two things died that day—shame and loneliness. And two childhood sweethearts got a second chance at life.

To Dance with an Angel

Sally and Connor were newlyweds. They still held hands, they still exchanged glances across the room, and each day still began and ended with a kiss. They loved to dance. It didn't matter if it was a town social or a spin around their tiny farmhouse floor. The music of love played in their hearts; they didn't need to hear it. Connor would take Sally's hand in the morning sunlight and twirl her around the kitchen. He told her she danced like an angel.

The thought of Connor leaving for war terrified his young wife. She begged him not to go. But Connor reassured her that everything would be all right. Those Yankees would be heading for home, sooner than later.

Connor searched the shops of Savannah for just the right keepsake to give to Sally. At last, he found it. It was expensive, but Connor would be earning some wages to send to Sally back home, and he asked the clerk to wrap it up for him.

As Sally unwound the ribbon, she saw a lovely wooden box with beautiful roses etched on top. She raised the lid, and a soft melody began to play. *"It is so beautiful, Connor. Every time I listen, I will send my heart to you."*

Connor left with his regiment the following week. The heat of summer was upon the troops. They all hoped they would be marching toward home again soon.

Sally put up a brave front, but inside, her heart was breaking. The days were lonely without Connor; the nights were even lonelier. She slept with one of his work shirts draped across his empty pillow. Tears were often soaked upon it.

It was a sunny July morning in 1861. Sally awoke to a stream of sunlight filling her bed. Upon the shelf, a small wooden box began to play. Sally looked up. The lid was still closed.

She grasped Connor's shirt and walked into the ray of sunshine. She danced one last time that morning with an Angel. Sally never danced again for the rest of her life.

What's for Dinner, Jack?

Jack was just eighteen when he enlisted. He was a likeable young man, making friends wherever he went. And so it was no surprise that Jack became a favorite among his fellow soldiers.

Most days were crummy; the conditions were horrendous. The ground was damp, the camp was filled with sickness, and the food sure wasn't enough to fill a hungry soldier's tired body. But Jack would lighten each meal around the campfire.

"What's for dinner tonight, Jack?" his buddies would ask.

"Let's see, tonight we are having mama's butter-drenched cornbread, with ham and gravy and some peach cobbler for dessert."

Though the soldiers sat around with bitter coffee and hardtack, their stomachs imagined the feast before them. Each night, Jack would announce the heavenly cuisine. As tired and sorrowful as he was, Jack never let a night go by without this mouth-watering commentary. And so it went, for months……

"What's for dinner, Jack?"

"Let's see, tonight there will be ribs, fresh buttered corn on the cob, fresh garden greens, and pecan pie for dessert."

Then a minie ball found Jack's stomach. He died instantly. His buddies dug a grave and one by one attended the funeral feast.

"Do you know what's for dinner tonight in heaven?" they asked.

"Let's see, there is all the sweet tea you can drink, all the ham, and ribs, and chicken, and fresh scrambled eggs, and hot, buttered biscuits......"

One by one, his buddies tossed dirt onto the grave and added to the menu.

"And strawberry rhubarb pie, and peach cobbler, and shoo fly pie, and trees tumbling over with ripe, sweet fruit in the orchards."

Without a single crumb of delicacy, they gave Jack a funeral feast. And that is truly what this kind and considerate boy deserved.

Clouds

J ake loved watching the sky since he was old enough to walk the acres of his family farm. He would sit and watch the clouds on lazy afternoons as a young boy—and on not-so-lazy afternoons, after chores were finished, as he grew older. Many times, he would tell his father to seek shelter for the horses and cows because a storm was coming. His brothers and sisters would gather round him as he told them stories about all the animals he saw in the sky.

It was no surprise that Jake would become the *cloud watcher* for his regiment. He could tell a lot from the clouds. Through bright, sunny skies, he could foresee the rain coming. He could warn of a dangerous storm. He could predict an early snow. And he could *see* things.

"Looks like it's going to be a tough battle. I see a wolf in the sky."

"Looks like those Rebs are gonna be sly as foxes today. Can you see that one staring down at us from the sky?"

At first, his buddies laughed his "sightings" off, but soon they *saw* the truth in Jake's prophecies. They learned to rely on them; the rigors of their marches and the timeliness of their encampments depended on his acute connection with the clouds. When Jake saw lambs, they felt at ease; perhaps the skirmish would be timid. When Jake saw a bear, the anxiety and fear rose among them.

One evening, Jake was unusually quiet. *"What did you see today in the clouds?"* his buddies asked. *"Must have been a cat, cause he's got Jake's tongue,"* one smirked. The chiding continued, but so did Jake's silence.

The next morning brought dark clouds, misty rain, and showers of bullets. They sailed through the sky like clouds. One found Jake. He lay on the field for several hours until the soldiers retrieved his body. He laid face upward, his open eyes still fixed on the sky above.

The sun was shining after the morning rain; only one fluffy cloud drifted overhead. Several soldiers thought it looked a lot like a young boy sitting on top, just gazing at the heavens......

"Farnsworth Angel"

"Sach's Bridge"

"Sallie Mae, the Loyal Pit Bull of Gettysburg"

"Horse"

"Kicking Up Dust"

"Rocking Chair"

"Irish Wolfhound"

"Old Dog"

"Vincent at Little Round Top"

Taking His Place

Robert was nineteen when he left his family's New York farm to enlist. He was a gifted boy; he had a way with animals on the farm. He seemed to connect with them, feel their pain when they were ill, and know their emotions as if they shared a human soul.

All the animals seemed to sense something was amiss the day Robert left. In later letters to her son, Robert's mother told him they hung their heads in a depressed manner, not eating or sleeping well for days.

Robert's mare, Lucy, was especially despondent. She no longer hurried to the gate for treats from Robert's loving hand. She seldom wandered the pasture, anxiously waiting by her same corner each day. It seemed she was off in a distant place, not on the farm fields, but in a sad world of her own. Robert's mother tried to comfort her, but only Robert could lighten the heaviness in Lucy's broken heart.

June 3, 1864 was a day of nightmares for Robert. It was Cold Harbor. The Union suffered terrible losses that day. By some miracle, Robert was spared, a fate not shared by so many of those he had grown to respect and love as brothers.

It was about a month later that Robert's mom got his letter. She had written to him, but she knew it would take some time for him to receive the news.

Lucy had lain down in the field and shut her heartbroken eyes on a quiet, summer day. It was June 3...perhaps a loving friend had taken Robert's place and exchanged her loving soul for his.

Going Home

It happened so quickly
One minute
running
Bayonet plunged forward.
The next
falling.
Blindness
Warmth
Rushing
down my head
Filling
my eyes......
Time stood still
War ended
All was dark
and quiet
My body sprawled
On the ground.
Time had no meaning
Day turned into night
Though I could not
see it,
I could
hear it.
Night peepers
I could
feel it.
Darkness'cold breeze
I could sense the stirrings of night creatures
in the woods

I heard moans
And screams
around me.

Boys calling for
Their mothers
Cries for water from parched mouths
Unable to scream
Only whisper softly
Perhaps one was my own voice
Whispering
in the night

Then light
Reached my eyes once again
I could stand.
I stumbled
Then
Braced myself
Against
a tree
And looked around
Soldiers
Carrying the wounded
Soldiers
Dragging the dead
Heaped into a trench

.

I searched for my canteen.
It was gone.

My letters from ma and Kathleen
Gone
Had they looted my body during the night?
The rocks hurt my feet
Then
I realized my shoes and socks
Gone
So much hurrying

No attention to me.
I asked for water
No one heard.

My shirt was caked with blood and dirt
I felt no pain.
I was lucky
The bullet missed me.
Not so for all my brothers
Their blood soaked me
Their dried blood caked my skin
I have to find my regiment.
My stride is strange
Lightness
Separation
Fill my body
Time and duty
Leave my thoughts
No rush
No pain

Then I see
A barefoot body
Dragged
Into the trench
His head half gone
I cannot see his face
until...
The next moment
in time

I am going home
But not to Massachusetts
Dear Mother

Seated with the Lord

ally was the house servant at Monroe Plantation, Mississippi. She was treated kindly, but Sally knew the horrors of slavery and feared for her future should something happen to the Monroe family.

She had helped raise Robert since he was born, caring for him through the nights when fever robbed him of restful sleep. She had three children of her own. Thankfully, they still lived at the plantation with her in a tiny slave shack.

Each evening, Sally would prepare the wonderful meal for Mr. and Mrs. Monroe, their two daughters, Emily and Amelia, and their son, Robert. The china was beautiful—not a chip. The glasses were sparkling, thanks to Sally's hands. The table was filled with the bounty of the fields and pastures.

Then war came. Times became harder. The table was still beautiful, but not as bountiful as before.

Robert became of age to join the Confederate Army. Both mothers were heartsick. Yes, *both* mothers. Mrs. Monroe and Sally, both mothers to this lanky-armed lad, too old to be a boy and too young to be a man, grieved at his departure.

Sally watched as he said goodbye to his family. She walked back into the kitchen, wiping a tear from her eye with her apron.

"You didn't think I'd forget my Sally," came a cheerful voice at the back door. *"Make sure you have some pie waiting for me when I come home."* Robert hugged her. Sally's heart swelled with happiness and sorrow at the same time, so much so she thought it would burst. *"Sure will, Master Robert."* Then, he was gone.

Mrs. Monroe was a superstitious woman. She had been raised by slaves who practiced the old religion and ways. *"Sally, make sure you place a setting for Robert each night at the family table."* So Sally did as she was told. Each evening, she placed a plate, silverware, glass, and napkin at Robert's place.

This continued for months. Robert's letters were infrequent; the family worries were constant—especially those of Mrs. Monroe. She faced each day in dread, worried that it might be her son's last.

Sally worked in the fields all morning after breakfast. She came in to prepare the family meal, then went home late in the evening to care for her own children. Their table was meager, but their love was abundant.

Sally knew the old ways too; her mother had taught her well. But she never shared this knowledge with Mrs. Monroe. One morning, while working in the fields, Sally saw

Robert. His image was fleeting, like a trick of the eye. But Sally knew……

She went in from the fields, made dinner, and set Robert's place. The perfect plate, the gleaming silverware, the pristine glass all in perfect position as usual. Then she went home. Dinner was humble—some cornbread, greens, a tiny piece of ham, and one sliver of pie. She carefully reached for her best bowl and set an extra place at the table.

"Who is this for, Mama?" her children asked. "Why can't we have the pie!!!?"

"It is for a special child of mine. He is having supper with our Lord tonight."

And so it was.

Soon after, the letter came. Robert's mother withdrew to her bedroom. She did not come down to meals anymore. Robert's place was never set again. But his place in Sally's heart was eternal.

Sorrow's Eclipse

I am the Moon
Full of quiet
And shadows

She is the Sun
Full of dancing
and Light

I hold my pencil and heart
By southern moonlight
She holds my letter and fear
In the northern sun

I dance with words
Hold the dead in my arms

She dances to music
Birdsong and fiddle

She gallops
On impulse

Grasps
The reins of the wind
In peaceful fields

The Gait of
My march
Steady and sure
In bullet ridden
Woods

She casts her light
My crescent moon
Smiles
Her slender grin
Softening
The darkened
Night

Now we are
Parted
My waxing moon
Full
Casting a glow
of
Sorrow

In the sky
Above
My
Heart.........

Dignity and Deception

Lawrence Talbot was a Pennsylvania youth still wet behind the ears when he joined his hometown regiment. He lived with his grandma, his mother, and his Aunt Lydia. His father had passed away some years back, but Larry was never really that close to him and, strangely, never suffered a son's grief.

Now, as he packed up his bag and blanket, his aunt stepped into his room. *"Lawrence, I need to talk to you before you leave. I had hoped this conversation would not take place for many more years, but I fear the time has come to speak now."* With a bewildered look on his face, Larry walked with his aunt onto the front porch and sat down.

"What is wrong, Aunt Lydia? You needn't worry; I will be all right and home before you know it."

But Lydia knew too many other young boys would never be home before they knew it. With tearful eyes, she struggled to find the right words.

Larry always wondered why Aunt Lydia had never married. All he knew of the family was that they had lived in Maryland until a short time before he was born. Then, his mother's mother in Pennsylvania had become ill and needed tending before she passed. So, the family moved back North. Larry, his mother, his father, and his Aunt Lydia all began a new life in Hanover, Pennsylvania.

"Lawrence, I am not your aunt. I am your mother."

Larry heard the words. They sailed inside his head like a small boat on the ocean, weaving up and down and trying to right itself. She continued before he got the word "what" out of his mouth.

"I was very young and fell in love with the neighbor's boy. We planned to be married, but there was bad blood between our families. My parents would not permit it. Soon after, I learned I was expecting a baby. My parents would not let me see this boy, would not let me tell him. They took me up North to my grandmother's house and told people the baby was my mother's and I was your aunt. I never saw your father again, and by the time I was old enough to escape my parents' constant supervision, I learned from a friend in Maryland he was engaged to another."

"Who is my father?"

"I will not tell you his name, for it will only bring sadness and unsettlement to his life. You bear his same blue eyes, though, and tall, lanky stride...although his leg was badly injured by a horse, and he was left with a limp to his walk in early youth."

Lawrence walked out of the house in a haze that morning. He didn't even say goodbye to his mother or "grandma" now.

Anger makes for a good soldier. Larry became quite skillful with his rifle. Whether aiming at real enemies or imagined demons inside his head and heart, his aim was never off. He became a sharpshooter and scout for the Union army. That is, until his luck ran out. He was captured on a scouting mission in Georgia.

Rebels led him to their encampment and to a large tent. Inside, a handsome General sat and sized this tall lad up with his piercing blue eyes.

"We could use a good scout like you. How would you like to work sharing information with us and save your Yankee skin at the same time?"

More deception was the last thing Lawrence could bear in his life; his answer was quick and sure.

"That's a shame," the General replied. *"Don't know what it is, but you remind me of someone. You have left me no choice but to send you to Andersonville."*

Larry knew of Andersonville. He knew it was a place that many walked into and never walked out of again. But Larry really didn't care. He felt like his whole life had been a lie. If death brought truth, then so be it. At least he would die with dignity, not with more deceit hung over his head.

The rebels led Larry out of the tent, hands tied. The General slowly sat up from his chair, limped over to the tent flap, and watched the young man being taken away.

Blackened Skies, Blackened Bodies
Gettysburg

Imagine how the smoke hung low
Above the rolling hills

The black flies swarmed
The fairer winged
Had left the skies
Quite still.

No birdsong
Only quiet moans
To rival cannon roar
The streams and creeks
Ran red with blood
And heinous battle gore.

Imagine when the rain
Poured down
To turn the fields to mud
And swollen bodies
Drenched in filth
And caked-on
Stench and blood.

Imagine all the horses
All the cows and pigs
And mules
Their rotted corpses
Scattered
Among the farmers'
Tools.

They say the smell

Still lingered
Come Autumn
Hard to bear
When Lincoln
Came to honor
Death's harvest
Of that year.

The Lady

Lucas was a southern boy, raised with the politeness and manners of a true gentleman. He was only eighteen years old when he joined the Confederacy. His gentle ways and congenial personality followed him, and soon, Lucas made many friends among his comrades in the 15th Alabama regiment.

His best friend, Jonas, often kidded him on his appearance. Through tousled hair and muddy shoes, Lucas tried to make the best of a slovenly appearance. *"A gentleman must always look his best,"* he'd tell his friend. Though torn and tattered, he would keep his clothes as best he could, and always keep his kepi firmly planted on his wind-tossed locks.

This July morning, Jonas noticed his friend wore no hat. *"Where is your kepi, Lucas?"* he chided with a grin.

"No kepi today, not with such a beautiful lady present," Lucas answered.

"What?" Jonas answered.

Lucas just repeated, *"I never wear a hat in the presence of a lady. She has come to see me home."*

Jonas was hot, he was tired, and he was worried about today's confrontation. He didn't have energy or desire to pursue the crazy ranting of his friend and chalked it up to no sleep and battle fatigue.

The regiment proceeded to a site known as Little Round Top. Guns, bayonets, chaos; the world was unraveling around them. Jonas lost track of his friend. It was only later when retreating down the hill that he saw his crumpled body beneath a large tree.

"Oh Lucas, my dearest friend." There was no time, no time to mourn or bury his friend. Only time to reach into his jacket pocket and put a crumpled kepi on his lifeless head. *"A gentleman must always look his best, especially on the way to the Lord,"* he whispered.

As he unfurled the kepi, a beautiful, white feather floated down upon Lucas' heart. Jonas picked it up and fled for his own life. He knew not why, but something in his own heart urged him to keep that feather, and when he reached a place of safety, he tucked it inside his Bible.

It was later that year, amidst the turning colors of the trees, that Jonas faced battle again at Chickamauga. It was here, surrounded by fire, that he saw them—a beautiful lady and a young, tousled hair boy waving at him by her side. They had come to see him home.

Many months later, among the effects that Jonas' family received, was a tattered and torn Bible—with one pristine, white feather tucked inside the page of the 23rd Psalm.

The Loyal Rat

Connor volunteered and joined the Confederacy when he was just seventeen. Hardly your usual soldier, Connor had something no other member of his regiment could claim. He had a pet rat. Yes, a little rat. Connor kept him in his shirt pocket. This rat was so spoiled that Connor's mother knitted him a little grey blanket to go along with the socks and vest she made for her beloved son.

At first, the other soldiers didn't take too kindly to a whiskered companion. But soon, they were sharing bits of hardtack and salt pork with him.

Squeakers would rise up each morning and stand at attention on top of Connor's head; he was quite the picture of a disciplined soldier. He kept his fur clean—rats are very clean you know. And he never strayed far from his master's side. He was a true friend.

Each night, Connor would write a letter to his mom, and Squeakers would nibble at the page corners. That was his way of sending hello.

When Connor got sick, he stayed cuddled on his chest to soothe the constant cough that took ages to heal.

Squeakers actually gained weight. He didn't march— he was carried. And he was constantly on the receiving end of any goodies parceled out to the regiment when mail came from back home. Fudge was his favorite, cookies a close second. All the other soldiers grew very fond of their tiny friend, and the affection was thoroughly reciprocated.

After about a year, Connor's regiment headed to a sleepy little Pennsylvania town. It was hot, so hot that Squeakers sought the shade of Connor's pocket for most of the day. He didn't like the loud noises constantly whizzing by his ears. His whiskers were very sensitive, and his nose detected a burning smell in the air.

Connor was a sharpshooter. He positioned himself behind a very large boulder and told Squeakers to keep hidden. Squeakers always did what Connor asked. He went to sleep in Connor's pocket, and when he woke, his friend lay very still.

Squeakers looked around. He recognized other friends who lay silently on the ground. Squeakers tried to lick Connor awake, but he didn't move. Sadly, Squeakers took his grey blanket out of Connor's breast pocket and curled up in it on his master's chest.

Days passed. Rain fell, and then, with the sun, came strange men searching through Connor's friends' pockets. Squeakers watched as these strange men took letters he had watched them read out of their pockets and toss them on the ground. He watched them take pocket watches and photos and tuck them inside their own pockets. Some carried large wooden sticks with handles and spoons on the ends. One tried to smash such a stick over Squeakers' head. Squeakers ran under a large rock, leaving his beloved friend and dropping his blanket behind. He watched the men load Connor onto a cart, along with his fellow soldiers.

Squeakers followed them as they came to a patch of ground and used their sticks to dig a large trench and toss the men inside. Squeakers was understandably frightened. He sniffed his way back to the boulders and searched the ground for his comforting blanket, carrying it in his mouth back to the freshly dug mound of dirt. He stayed there for the night, crying for his friends. The following morning, his tummy rumbled for a piece of hardtack, but there was none.

He made a nest back in the boulders. He spent the rest of summer there. Then autumn came. The smells still lingered in the air that burned his tiny nostrils. He wandered through the fields in search of food and watched men preparing a big memorial. They worked with those same giant spoons and dug graves for many, many soldiers.

Squeakers wondered why his friends had been forgotten. Each day, he collected wildflowers and brought them to the place where their bodies had been tossed. No mother would know where her son lay buried, but Squeakers would never forget.

Soon, autumn drifted into winter, and the weather became very cold for an aging rat. No more food could be found, no more wildflowers grew in the fields. Squeakers missed the warmth of Connor's pocket, the fudge, the cookies, and the special treat of warm milk the soldiers took from farmers' cows every once in a while.

His grey blanket had grown thin and tattered, but he carried it this December morning to the spot where Connor lay. He curled on top of this forgotten mound of soil and closed his eyes for the last time, a loyal soldier until his final breath.

The Wind

He marched
The wind at his back
The smell of jasmine
Gardenia
Magnolias
Send it to her, he whispered to the wind
Send her the fragrance, send her my love
He marched
The wind out of the east
Rain pelting down on his jacket
Soaking his face
Hiding his tears
The smell of wet grass
Soaked fields
Send it to her, he whispered to the wind
Send her my tears
Tell her I miss her
He marched
The wind of storms
Swirling around him
As his body fell upon the ground
His soul lifting
Lifting with the wind
Send it to her, he whispered to the wind
Send me home

Guardian Ghost

Dogs and country boys go hand in hand. Such was the way it was for Todd and Spot. The lanky youth and the big, floppy-eared mutt were inseparable. More than once, Spot had gotten Todd out of some risky situations. One such time, he pulled the boy out of a fishing hole by the hem of his overalls, tugging until he was sure his friend was on dry land.

Spot was big and strong, and he was always holding Todd back from danger. Once, when Todd fell out of Neighbor Parker's oak tree and sprained his ankle, Spot ran all the way home, barking wildly. Good thing Todd's father followed him back to that tree, or Spot would have dragged Todd the entire mile back to his farmhouse. That's just the way it was with them; never a day passed that Spot wasn't keeping court as Todd's shadow and protector.

Years passed. The brown muzzle of Spot's face turned grey. His gait stiffened a bit, but his tail wagged just as strongly each time Todd walked in the door. Todd was away more and more now; he had chores and jobs to do. One day, Spot watched his friend pack a bag filled with socks, a woolen blanket, and an extra shirt and pair of pants. He watched as Todd slung it over his shoulder and sat quietly as his friend bent down to pat him on the head and say, *"Goodbye, old boy. I will miss you."*

Spot's heart broke that day. He spent most of the days that ensued just sleeping by the front porch, hoping for a glimpse of a lanky figure returning home in the distance. Weeks passed, then months. Finally, Spot's fragile heart gave out, and he left this earth one sunny spring morning.

That same morning, Todd and his regiment were embroiled in a fierce battle. What started as gunfire turned into deadly hand-to-hand combat. As his fellow soldiers marched forward, Todd felt a sharp tug on his pants leg, a tug so strong it knocked him to the ground. He saw his friends' bodies shattered as minie balls flew through the air. He watched others land around and on top of him. Todd struggled to get up, but it felt like a one hundred pound weight was lying on top of him, shielding him from the fray.

Todd was covered in blood. He thought surely he had been hit, and his body was failing him. That must be the reason he could not stand up. But when the battle was over, Todd could stand up. He could walk. He could run to safety. He was not wounded.

Todd made it back to camp safely. Letters did not come for weeks from home. When a letter finally arrived, it told of the sad, spring morning Todd's mom found Spot lying lifeless on the ground.

"He was such a good boy, always shielding you from harm," she wrote.   Then, Todd remembered that spring morning when the weight of the world—or one very large dog—seemed to lay on his body. Could it have been? Maybe, just maybe, one more time, an old friend had come to keep his master safe from harm.

"Goodbye, old boy. I will miss you. Thanks."

Blossoms in the Snow

It was late summer when John kissed his young bride goodbye and left to join the Union Army.

It was early in the morning, and the hint of fall whispered in the cool breeze that swayed the leaves above their heads. Ellen had packed his sparse possessions and put the last of the summer fruit in his knapsack for him to enjoy. As they walked together down the path of their tiny home, John picked the last of the fading rose blossoms off a little bush.

"Don't worry, Ellen. By the time spring comes, I'll be home again to pick you a fresh blossom."

Ellen smiled and waved goodbye. She prayed his words were true.

As months passed, she wrote John every night. She wrote of the turning leaves. She told him of the reds and oranges and golds. She wrote of apple cider and harvested crops, of the crisp smell of fall in the air.

John wrote her of strange moss hanging from the trees, of swamps, and of wilderness.

Autumn turned to winter. John began to wonder if this war would ever end, if spring back at his little home would ever happen.

Ellen wrote of snow, of frosty breath lingering in the air, of piney fragrance in the wind. Their little rose bush was just a tangle of twigs and thorns in the snow now.

Spring came. John didn't come home. The rose blossoms came, but John didn't. Ellen picked the petals, placed them in her letters to him, and wept.

Months passed. The roses gave way to apples and harvests. The harvests invited winter again, but still no John. He had seen many battles, more deaths than he could blind from his mind and heart.

It was an especially harsh winter up north. Ellen struggled to make it to the post office to send John his letters. Then, his letters stopped. Weeks passed......

"It must be the weather. The snow has slowed the mail," she thought. But she worried, and she wept.

One February morning, Ellen dressed warmly and started down the path to the post office. Her eyes met something red in the snow. There, in the tangle of twigs and thorns, bloomed one red rose. Ellen dropped to her knees, tears rolling down her cheeks, as she gazed upon the blossom at her snow-laden boots. Her neighbor found her weeping in the snow, amazed to see a rose bloom in her hands.

A lifetime passed. A lifetime of summers, autumns, winters, and springs. Ellen's tiny rose bush blossomed into a towering cascade of blossoms.

John's body was never found. Ellen hoped to lay his body to rest, but in her heart, she knew he had come home. A little rose had told her so, a February blossom that meant more to her heart than a lifetime of spring bouquets.

Sounds

He heard the cannons rumble
She missed the sound of his voice

He heard the screams of pain in the night
She missed his laughter in the morning sun

He heard the horses whinnying in fear
She missed the way he whistled for his dog

He heard the bugles call to reveille
She missed his fiddle by the fire

He heard the angels call to him
She missed what might have been

She heard the war was over
She missed all joy that day

Socks of Love

Teddy was just a boy when he packed up his sparse bag and told his mother he was leaving to join the Union Army. It was just Teddy and his mom. He was the light that shone in her morning sun each day. He was spoiled as best as a poor hard-working farmer's wife could spoil him. She cooked all his favorites; she baked all the treats her meager ingredients could manage.

But meager ingredients didn't matter—Sarah's cakes and cookies and fudge were the best in town. Others would flock to her place at the church Sunday dinner table to see what temptations she brought inside her basket of breads and sweets. Everyone in town loved Sarah, not just for her baking, but for her heart. Sarah said it was the heart that baked, not the sugar or flour or eggs. That was why her desserts always came out perfectly. And, after one bite of Sarah's chocolate fudge or sugar cookies, it was hard to dispute.

Sarah packed those sugar cookies in a tattered bag this morning and watched her son walk off. She didn't cry, at least not until he was far down the path. Her spoiled little boy, how would he manage in this horrible war.......

Teddy needed to prove he wasn't a boy any longer—he was a man. He had been teased for so long about being mama's little boy that this war seemed the perfect place to show his stuff. So, along with a few other boys in town, he had signed up as a volunteer.

It wasn't easy for Teddy. Camp meals sure weren't the same as at home. Those hard biscuits couldn't hold a candle to one of Sarah's *melt-in-your-mouth* clouds of dough. But when mail was called, Teddy and his mates flocked to his package as fast as those Sunday churchgoers had. What was it today? Chocolate fudge? Pound cake? Molasses cookies? It didn't matter. Whatever was in that parcel, it was a little piece of home, of heaven, of mama's heart. Teddy always shared; he only left himself a few cookies or a small piece of whatever treat his mama packed. He knew how much it meant to all his friends, suffering the same as he was each day through the horrors of war.

As months passed, the cookies went further, the pieces of fudge were bigger. There were fewer boys to share them with, as war had claimed so many lives. Teddy wrote faithfully to his mom, telling her how delicious everything was. Even when mud and rain had soaked through and ruined her dessert, Teddy never mentioned this, only saying how all the soldiers had raved about her baking.

Sometimes, Sarah mailed hand-knitted socks to Teddy. Special socks they were, for placed inside were her delicious sugar cookies. The other soldiers were fooled at first by these packages. *"Only socks,"* they would say. But kind-hearted Teddy shared the secret contents within the wool and would only leave a couple of cookies inside for himself as he placed the socks inside his uniform pocket.

Fierce fighting took Teddy's life one sunny morning. Half of his face had been shattered away, and he lay broken on the bloody field. His buddies lay around him all through the night, until the next day when a Confederate soldier picked through his pockets. A smile of happiness crossed his face when he discovered the socks in Teddy's pocket. Oh, how his bloody, shoeless feet ached for a pair of socks! As he opened them to put them on, a few broken cookies fell to the ground. The soldier could not believe his good fortune. He picked them up and ate them in quick bites.

Then, he cried. He cried for what he had become, for what the war had turned him into. Just for a moment. That was all the time war gave for crying. But before he left, he thanked a boy whose face, now gone, would never hear his thanks. A boy who had made another soldier feel human again, if only for a moment.

Sarah kept sending packages for weeks, but she did not hear from Teddy. Then, news came to her town about the regiment. War casualties were posted.

Sarah never baked again. She said it took heart to make a cookie, or bread, or lighter-than-air biscuits. She said her heart was gone now.

A few years later, Sarah joined her son. The church held a beautiful service. The ladies of the congregation baked their best. And indeed it was their best, for grieving hearts were a most important ingredient.

From a Soldier's Heart

I miss my little dog
I miss the brave soldier
Who marched on furry paws
Following on the field
Barking at morning call
Being grateful for whatever scrap
Was tossed his way

I miss his soft fur
Warming me at night
I miss his warm tongue
Licking at my sore and
Bloodied feet

I miss the ears
That heard my whispers
His heart
That beat for me
Just me...

Just him and me......
That's all we had
No kin
No friends
That's why we joined
He didn't ask, just
Followed......

Followed until the end
When he sat
Looking in my eyes

Eyes filled with fear
Knowing we would part

My heart said goodbye this morning
To the dearest friend I ever knew

You see, this morning
I died
I watched my friend through
Spectred eyes

He wouldn't leave my side for
Many hours......
Finally, he walked into the woods

He came upon a little farm
A girl played in the fields

She scooped him in her arms
And took him in the barn

I might have burned that barn
If I had lived

My enemy has taken my truest friend
And offered love

Sad, how war makes enemies of friends
And death makes friends of enemies

My heart and spectred eyes leave now
Farewell my little dog
I loved you
Now others will too
Our war is over.

A Mother's Voice

Quiet nights
His ears rung
Eardrums trembling
Remembering
Minie balls and bullets

He tried to
Think of tree peepers
Crickets
Cows mooing
Softly in the
Barn

Young
But old beyond his years
He only knew death
Remembering
His mother's ashen face
Still across her bed
His little body trembling
He called her name
She had no voice

Remembering the silence

He could not remember
The sound of her voice
That saddened him
He heard the soldiers
Cry out to their mothers
Their weak voices
Remembering
Their wounded bodies
Trembling with fear

He still could see her face
In his head
And in the glaring sun
As he marched
His feet bloody and filled
With pain
Was it a trick of his mind
Or was she there
Remembering her son?

The day was quiet now
He could not hear
The bullets, the cannon
He could not see his buddies
The worry in their eyes
The blood on his chest
But he could see her face
In his closed eyes
And remember her voice
As it called to clasp
His trembling hand in hers......

Gettysburg Rain

Rain lingers in footprint puddles
In the mud
On the battlefield
Are these the prints of camera-toting tourists
Running for shelter
Or
Perhaps
Soldiers
Stuck in time
Like prints stuck in muddied fields
When bullets fell
Like rain from the sky
Through the trees
And soldiers fell
And became part of this Hallowed Ground
Forever
Running for shelter......

Epilogue

I am honored to be the guardian of a historic Civil War farmhouse in Gettysburg.

Should you ever have the privilege to walk the hallowed grounds of Gettysburg or another sacred battlefield, think of all the fallen who left a piece of their soul or a piece of their body on these fields. Remember those who never made it home again.

But also think of those left behind. Imagine the tears of mothers, wives, fathers, and children who waited for a loved one to walk through a door that never ushered a welcome against its threshold again. Imagine the ones who survived and bore guilt that haunted for the remainder of their lives.

I cannot fully explain by mere words, but I hope my stories have shed a glimmer into the hearts of all who lived and died in this time of war between brothers, families, and friends. I cannot replicate the true emotions—only try to reenact them from my heart.

Coda

I never knew my Uncle Ralph. Though I knew him in spirit, I always felt close to him. Another medium told me he lingered around me. That made sense. As a young girl, war always fascinated me. I would sneak into my brothers' bedroom and carry off war books. I would sit and watch war series on television and war movies while others were watching sitcoms.

Ralph was exceptionally gifted with mathematics; he had been accepted to West Point, but the draft took him to Europe. Uncle Ralph was nineteen years of age when he died in the Ardennes Forest at the Battle of the Bulge. I have the scrap of paper telegram that was sent to the family. That scrap must have torn my grandma's heart into tiny pieces. She left this world soon after.

I always think about his absence—the cousins I never had, the uncle I never got to know. Each year, we visit his grave on Memorial Day, instead of his home and family.

I hope these stories make an uncle proud of the niece he never got to meet, only watch over from the spirit world.

The author shares her Gettysburg farmhouse with a pack of furry friends. Pictured here is Aura Lea, her Irish Wolfhound.

Information about Shirl's Reiki and intuitive work is featured at: www.briarrosereiki.com.

Her art and photography gallery link is:
http://shirlknoblochwillowfineartprintsandphotography.zenfolio.com/

Shirl also writes regularly on three blog pages:

https://walkingamongtheghostsofgettysburg.wordpress.com/

https://wordpress.com/stats/day/sknobloch88.wordpress.com
(The Roses and Thorns of Life)

https://wordpress.com/stats/day/tenleggedjourney.wordpress.com